Another Dance

A
California Belly Dance Romance
Sexy Short Story

Book 3

Another Dance

A
California Belly Dance Romance
Sexy Short Story

Book 3

DEANNA CAMERON

Fine Skylark Media
California

Fine Skylark Media
P.O. Box 1505
Lake Forest, California 92609-1505

Another Dance
Copyright © 2015 DeAnna Cameron
ISBN-13: 978-0-9908146-3-4

Cover photography by Vintra via Depositphoto.com (dancer) and Illustrated Romance (male model)

TITLES BY DEANNA CAMERON

PRAISE FOR *SHIMMY FOR ME*

"DeAnna Cameron delivers satisfying happily ever afters that will leave you sighing."
—Beth Yarnall author of *Wake Up Maggie*

"Cameron ensures that love triumphs in a delightful and believable way."
—Susan Squires, New York Times bestselling author of the Magic series

PRAISE FOR *THE BELLY DANCER*

"A beautifully written page-turner with characters that leap off the page, *The Belly Dancer* transports readers into an exotic and sensual world within a world, as plucky but initially naive Dora Chambers fights Chicago society's conventions and her husband's indifference to discover, in the thrall of the Egyptian Theatre, a passion beyond her wildest dreams."
—Lynette Brasfield, author of *Nature Lessons: A Novel*

"The 1893 World's Fair was a marvel, and in her debut, Cameron uses this backdrop to demonstrate one woman's view of herself. Society is forever altered because of what she learns in the lush, sensual, and exotic world of belly dancers. With a strong and vibrant picture of the era and a feminist approach to history, Cameron makes statements about women's rights and society's constraints."

—RT Book Reviews (4 stars)

PRAISE FOR *DANCING AT THE CHANCE*

"Old New York comes to vibrant life in this dazzling tale of follies and illusions. *Dancing at The Chance* serves up a racy, exuberant feast for the senses, with a lively and intrepid heroine determined to succeed in a fading world threatened by fast-paced, fickle modernity."

—C.W. Gortner,
author of *The Confessions of Catherine de Medici*

"*Dancing at The Chance* took me back to Old New York, when vaudeville still enchanted audiences and Ziegfeld was king. In her second novel, DeAnna Cameron brings the world of 1900's theatre to vibrant life. Part circus, part Shakespeare, part Arabian nights, the Chance Theatre is a place I would love to visit again."

—Christy English, author of *To Be Queen*

DEDICATION

To the readers who asked to keep the bedroom door
open. You know who you are.

CHAPTER ONE

A SOUND AT the door pulled Taz Roman from his hazy morning thoughts. Instantly alert, he grabbed the bed sheet and pulled it over Melanie's bare shoulders and his own naked body before the familiar silhouette was in the room.

"Mr. Roman! Oh dear, I didn't know you were home."

The short, round woman with her hair wrapped beneath a scarf shielded her eyes from the sleeping couple.

"It's all right, Anna," Taz said, trying not to move so he didn't disturb Melanie, who was lying on his chest. He looked to see if she was awake, but her eyes were closed, and her chest rose and fell in the gentle rhythm of slumber. "The party ran late last night, so we took a cab home."

"Shall I give you a few minutes?" she asked, turning toward the hallway.

He glanced at Melanie again. This time one eyelid was lifted and she was peering at him, dazed and half-conscious. She shook her head.

"Maybe you should skip this room," he said to Anna. "We might be a while."

"We?" Confused, Anna turned back and noticed Melanie. She whirled away again. "I had no idea. I'm so sorry. Of course. I'll be downstairs. You just... Well, I—"

"It's all right, Anna," he said with a chuckle. "Thank you."

Without another word, his housekeeper pulled the door closed behind her.

"That's a first," Melanie said after a yawn. "I've never been awakened by a maid before."

"Sorry about that. I should have left her a note downstairs, but I wasn't exactly thinking about the housekeeping last night."

Melanie moaned in that deep, sexy way of hers and wound her legs more tightly around his.

"I hope not," she said. "I was trying very hard to keep your attention on me."

Feeling her bare skin and her heat against him brought it all back. First, killing it onstage at the Belly Dance Divas' premiere. Easily his best opening night performance ever. Being out there with his drum as Melanie danced made it the most incredible opening night ever. From the moment they'd stepped off that stage, all he'd wanted to do was get her into the dressing room and lock the door.

He might have managed it, too, if Garrett hadn't already been in the wings, bragging about the after party he'd arranged. Taz would have skipped it, but Melanie refused. It was her first big show and the official launch of the show's ten-week world tour. She told him she didn't want to miss anything, including the after parties. Then she'd nibbled his ear and promised there'd be time for everything else later.

Later had turned out to be three in the morning.

By the time the cab had delivered them home and they'd stumbled through his front door, they'd barely made it to the bedroom.

But they hadn't even made it to the bedroom, had they?

A quick rummage for food in the kitchen had turned into something else entirely. He imagined the look on Anna's face when she discovered the streaks of whipped cream on the kitchen island that had been left when Melanie emptied the can in her creative—and incredibly seductive—use of that frothy sweet topping. And then there were the clothes they'd stripped off and left on the floor before running upstairs for a shower that was supposed to clean them up but had turned fifty shades of dirty instead.

A satisfied grin stretched across his face at the memory of it.

By the time they'd actually made it to bed, they'd both collapsed with exhaustion.

He tugged again at the sheet and adjusted his head against the pillow. It had been one hell of a night in so many ways, and now with Melanie sprawled over him, it was the perfect morning. He brushed his fingertips across her arm and her hair, enjoying her softness and her warmth.

How in the world had he gotten so lucky?

"Damn," she said, interrupting his thoughts. "I didn't bring an overnight bag. I don't have anything with me."

"I'm right here. What else could you possibly need?"

She slapped his chest playfully.

"A toothbrush, for starters. A decent hairbrush, a flat iron. Shall I go on?"

"You don't need that stuff, and we've got all day. Besides, the car service will be here before dawn tomorrow to pick us up for the airport, so you might as well sleep while you can. It's only nine."

"It's already nine?" She shot up and rubbed her eyes. "You shouldn't have let me sleep so late. I've never packed for a tour before. I have a million things to do."

He slid his hand up her thigh. "Relax. The only thing you have to do is me."

He worked his fingers between her legs.

She kissed the top of his head but wiggled out of reach.

"As appealing as that sounds, I can't stay." She dropped her head back and groaned. "And my mom will be up by now, which means on top of everything else, I get to start the day with a walk of shame."

He traced figure eights in the bed sheet. "You know, you wouldn't if your things were already here."

"What do you mean? Like an extra toothbrush?"

"Yeah. A toothbrush, or maybe all your stuff. There's plenty of room."

Too much room. Lately, that's how it felt when she wasn't around. Sharing his house with her when she was his fake girlfriend had changed everything. Now it only felt like home when she was in it.

The horrified look on her face, however, made it clear she didn't feel the same.

"Please tell me you didn't just ask me to move in with you. That would be insane. My mom needs me, and seriously, how would that even work?"

His brain went numb. He stared at the sheet, at the wall, at anything but her as he tried to think of something to say. Because she was right. It was a stupid idea. It was insane. Right? He wanted to say so but the blow to his gut was making it difficult to get the words out. He managed a shrug. "Of course I'm kidding."

She hit him with a pillow. "Like I'd move in with you. Do you think I'm crazy?"

She was laughing.

He tried to laugh, too, and grabbed the next pillow she had aimed at him. "I definitely don't think you're crazy," he said softly. He locked glances with her, and he wanted to say more. For a split second he thought maybe he should say what he was really feeling. That he'd never been happier than he'd been these past few weeks. That he couldn't imagine his life without her.

But what if she laughed at that, too?

He dropped the pillow on the bed and turned away, debating what to say or whether to say anything. He opted to say nothing. Instead, he rose, and pulled a fresh pair of boxers from the dresser. "You're right," he said, stepping into the shorts and yanking them up. "It's late. We should get moving."

Melanie frowned. "You're leaving?"

"Yeah. I don't know what I was thinking. I've got a ton of stuff to do. I have to swing by the drum shop and the office. Check on the instruments to make sure everything gets packed right. I don't need any broken drums in London." He ticked off several more small and tedious tasks—tasks he'd already delegated to a tour assistant. Since he needed someplace else to be right now, he might as well attend to them himself.

"When do you think you'll be back?" Melanie asked.

"I don't know. This stuff could take a while." It was going to take all day and then some, if he could manage it.

The creases around her mouth deepened. "But don't you have to pack?"

"I'm done. Mostly. You know, we don't have to go to the airport together. I can have Garrett send a car to your mom's place."

Her brown eyes locked onto his green ones. "But I want to go together. I just have to get a few things. I told my mom I'd spend the day with her, but I can be back before dinner. You know, if you want to grab something later."

He shrugged, like it made no difference. "Sure. Fine." He opened a dresser drawer and rummaged for a clean T-shirt.

"How about seven-thirty?" she asked. "Wait, seven would be better."

Her voice cracked with a hint of emotion, and it twisted his insides. His conscience told him to wrap his arms around her and tell her everything was all right. He just couldn't. Not yet.

"Don't worry about Anna," he said. "Stick around as long as you want. She won't get in your way. See you later." He grabbed his wallet from the top of the dresser and headed for the door.

"Hey, wait. You don't have your Jeep. My car's still parked on the street. I can drive you back to the club."

"No," he said. "I'll get a cab. Don't worry about it."

By then, Melanie was off the bed and shuffling toward him with the sheet wrapped around her. She stopped in front of him, rose to her tiptoes, and wrapped one arm around his neck. "Well, you can't leave without a kiss."

He leaned down and quickly pecked her lips.

She shook her head, tightened her arm around his neck, and held him closer, pressing her lips against his and waiting for him to soften.

He didn't want to give in, but, damn. Being this close to her, feeling her skin and smelling the warm, clean scent of her, he lost his resolve. His hands wound around her waist as if they had a mind of their own. He pressed her against him and gave in to her deep, ardent kiss.

But then, in his mind, he saw her horrified look again. "That would be insane," echoed in his mind and pierced his pride again. He pulled back.

"I'll see you later," he said, turned, and disappeared down the hall.

CHAPTER TWO

MELANIE WATCHED THE closed door for a full minute before she moved. Had he really just walked out on her? Part of her thought he was going to stick his head back in, and with that big, celebrity smile of his, say, "Just kidding!"

But he didn't. He wasn't going to, either. The deepest, most honest part of herself knew he was gone, and it was because of her stupid, careless mouth.

She'd done it again: she'd ruined everything. She could feel it in his kiss, and she could see it in his eyes when he pulled away.

This was the most incredible guy she'd ever known and probably the best relationship she'd ever had, and she'd blown it. Plain and simple.

The worst part was, she knew he'd been serious when he'd asked her to move in. It just scared the crap out of her. Each day with him felt like an amazing gift, and she was loving every minute of it. She didn't want anything to change it.

The few weeks they'd been together since he'd walked into the Shimmy Shop and invited her to be the featured dancer during his drum solos had been the best weeks of her life. Not just because she was finally a member of the Belly Dance Divas touring dance troupe, her dream job and then some, but because she was doing it with him.

He was everything she'd ever wanted in a guy. He got her in a way nobody else ever had. He laughed at her jokes and understood her moods. She never had to explain herself to him. It made her laugh to remember the self-absorbed playboy she'd assumed him to be. But then, she knew better than most how wrong first impressions could be.

When he was with her, he was sweet and funny and always a gentleman. And the way he could make her feel. No one had ever made her feel like that. Ever.

Experience told her that kind of magic couldn't last.

And once they were on the road, everything would be different anyway.

Maybe it was better this way.

CHAPTER THREE

MELANIE STOOD OUTSIDE the door of her mom's single-wide trailer in the Bella Garden Mobile Home Park and listened. The drone of the television seeped through the wood. She glanced down at the T-shirt she'd taken from Taz's dresser and could already hear her mother's snide comments. She closed her eyes. She should probably be ashamed, but she didn't have the energy. Instead, she straightened, pulled her shoulders back, and turned the knob.

"There you are," Ginger Drake said from the recliner that filled most of the front room. Her right foot was bandaged and propped on a stool. The typical cola can sat on the table beside her. "I was wondering when you'd come home."

"I know. I should have called or let you know I was staying out. But it got late. I didn't want to wake you."

Ginger shook her head. "Of course you were out late. After that performance, you deserve to celebrate. Honey, you were beautiful out there. More than beautiful. You were the best thing on that stage."

Her mom beamed like she did when she solved the Wheel of Fortune puzzle before the contestants.

"Thanks," Melanie said, confused by her mother's reaction. "I think the audience liked it. But you didn't miss much. There'll be other shows."

She'd made peace with the doctor's order that Ginger stay off the foot for at least six weeks after the surgery. The bunion had been particularly nasty, and they'd been lucky to find a doctor who was even willing to operate on a payment plan, considering her mother's lack of insurance. Of course Mom had wanted to delay the procedure until after the show, but Melanie had insisted her health came first. Ginger needed to get that foot fixed before she could get off that recliner and on with her life.

Still, it had been a disappointment to know her mother wouldn't be in the audience.

"I know there'll be other shows, but you didn't think I was really going to let some quack tell me I couldn't see my own daughter's big debut, did you?"

Melanie frowned. "You didn't. Did you? Really?"

"Of course I did," Ginger said. From the cushion crevice, she pulled out a ticket stub. "Balcony, row D, seat 1."

"But you shouldn't have," Melanie said, feeling guilty and happy at the same time. "The doctor said so."

"I didn't do anything more strenuous than walking to the bathroom and back. I even used those damned crutches you made me get." She thrust her chin at the pair leaning behind the door. "Once I got to the theater, a young man at the front brought me a wheelchair and steered me all the way to my seat. He even came to help me when it was over. He was very nice, though I'm sure he was just angling for a tip."

"You did tip him, right?"

"Of course. Two dollars."

Melanie shook her head but didn't say anything. No matter what, her mother tipped two dollars. No more, no less. Instead of trying again to explain that tipping expectations had changed since the 1970s, she went to the recliner, bent down, and threw her arms around her mom.

"Oh, oh!" her mom exclaimed, surprised, then delighted.

A soft tapping on Melanie's back let her know her mother was embracing her, too. After a long moment, Melanie pulled away.

"Thank you. I wish you would have told me you were going to be there. I could have gotten you backstage. You could have met everyone."

"No," Ginger scoffed. "I didn't want that. That was your time. I wanted you to enjoy it. The last thing you needed to think about was your invalid mother."

"Temporarily invalid, and still, that's not true. It would have been nice to introduce you to some people."

"Like that young man playing the drum?"

"Yeah, like him," she said, blushing despite herself. "His name's Taz."

Ginger grabbed the television remote and muted the sound.

"So that's the famous Taz Roman. The special guy you've been spending so much time with lately."

Melanie rose and turned away. "The one and only." She tried to keep her voice even.

"He's certainly handsome. At least what I could see from the balcony. But since he wasn't wearing much under that vest of his, I could see quite a lot."

Melanie flushed again. "Yeah, he's pretty great. Do you want another soda?"

"Melanie Jean, you aren't trying to change the subject, are you?"

"No," she said, lying.

"I'd say he must be special if he's been keeping you so busy."

"We've been rehearsing." Mostly, anyway. These past few weeks had been special. Maybe more than special. At least until she'd gone and blown it.

"Now you'll be off together, traipsing around the world with this show of yours. I hope you're going to behave yourself."

She shot a look at her mom, but Ginger was smiling.

"I mean," her mom added with a sly grin, "don't do anything I wouldn't do."

That was all she could take. Melanie covered her face with both hands, and the tears she'd been holding back burst through.

"Hey, hey," her mom said. "I was joking. I know you won't be foolish."

Melanie swiped at her tears. She felt foolish now. She hadn't cried in front of her mother since... she couldn't even remember the last time. And now, over a guy? But Taz wasn't just a guy. He was... more.

"Come here, baby girl. Tell me what happened."

The nickname startled her. Her mother hadn't used it since she was little, when she'd come home crying over some slight at school or a lost doll. But it still soothed her, just as it had then. She walked back to the recliner, kneeled again, and rested her forehead on the recliner's arm.

"I already ruined everything, Mom."

Her mother's fingers stroked the top of her head.

"I doubt that. Even from the balcony, I could see the way he looked at you. I don't think you ruined anything."

"But I did. Me and my big, fat mouth. This morning he asked me to move in with him, and I laughed at him."

Ginger didn't say anything, and Melanie didn't dare lift her head to see the look on her face.

"It was awful," Melanie continued. "I thought he was joking, so I laughed. But everything I said to make up for it just made it worse."

"Are you sure you thought he was joking? Or was it something else?"

Melanie glanced up. Her mother stared back, unflinching.

"What do you mean?"

Ginger shrugged. "Maybe nothing."

But she knew her mother was insinuating something.

"You think I did it on purpose, don't you?"

"I didn't say that," Ginger said.

"I mean, it probably doesn't make any difference. After tomorrow everything will be different anyway.

We'll be in airports and hotels and theaters, and he'll have all those girls throwing themselves at him."

Last night alone, how many times had eager and beautiful fans clamored for his attention? They begged for autographs and photographs and who knew what else when she was out of earshot. It was a brutal awakening to what life was going to be like on the road.

Her mother continued to stroke her hair. Then, after a long and silent moment, she said, "You probably did yourself a favor. He's nice enough to look at, but maybe that's all there is. If you can't trust him, maybe you're better off letting him go."

Melanie's head shot up. "I wouldn't be better off, and he's not just nice to look at. He is, yeah, but he's also sweet and kind. He's honest and thoughtful. He opens doors for me, Ma. He cooks."

"If you can't trust him—"

"But I didn't even give him a chance."

A soft, gentle smile spread across the usually hard lines of Ginger's face. "Well, there you are. It sounds like you know what to do."

Melanie dropped her head back on the armrest. "You didn't see the way he looked at me this morning. Just blank, like it was already over."

"I doubt that," her mother said. "If this is as bad as you say and if he's the man you say he is, then I really don't know why you're wasting time here. Go and fix this."

CHAPTER FOUR

ANNA WAS HUMMING TO herself and scrubbing the kitchen sink when Melanie walked back into Taz's house. The woman turned, saw Melanie, and became flustered all over again.

"Mr. Roman isn't home. I'm not sure when he's going to be back."

"Actually, I was hoping he'd still be gone," Melanie said hesitantly, still unsure exactly what she intended to do.

"Oh. If you need the room then, just let me rinse this and get these out of your way." Anna pulled the faucet's spray nozzle to rinse the cleanser down the drain, then wiped her hands on her apron and grabbed the plastic carryall that held an assortment of spray bottles, jars, and scrubbers.

"Wait," Melanie said when the woman was halfway to the door. "Can I ask you something?"

Anna stopped and straightened. "Of course, dear. What can I do for you?"

Melanie opened her mouth but a flurry of tiny yips and barks from the other room stopped her.

"Oh, Spikey, leave her alone, lass," Anna hollered in the general direction of the noise.

Melanie tried again, but the barking erupted again, even more ferocious than before.

"That's it, no more!" Anna threw up her hands and left the room.

Melanie followed. She watched Anna scoop up Spike, who was doing her best throaty growl at a black cat staring at her from the other side of the glass.

"Don't you let that kitty cat make you crazy," Anna said, stroking Spike's head. Only when she closed the blinds and the cat was out of view did the dog calm down.

"I swear that cat taunts her on purpose just to make a fuss," Anna said. "It's okay, Spiky. She's gone now. You've done your job. We're safe."

When they were back in the kitchen, Anna deposited Spike at her bowl, and the dog lapped at the water.

"Guarding the house from the neighbor's cat is a thirsty business," Melanie said.

"Oh, you have no idea," Anna said, chuckling. "It's become a daily battle of wills. But enough of that. What were you going to say, dear?"

Melanie settled into one of the chrome stools at the island. She touched the place where she'd lain the night before, and the memory of it all slipped back. The bumping and the grinding and the whipped cream. A mortifying heat crept up her neck. She glanced around for the cream's residue and found nothing but gleaming stainless steel. They had not left it that way. She definitely remembered that. She dropped her glance to the floor and felt another rush of heat across her cheeks

"Don't worry about all that, dear," Anna cajoled. "It was no problem at all. In fact, I'm quite pleased to see you and Mr. Roman are having such a… good time together. It's been quite a while since he's brought anyone home, you know."

The woman's soft Scottish lilt gave her words a reassuring sweetness.

"Really?" Melanie said, peeking up beneath the ridge of her eyebrows. "He doesn't bring anyone here?"

Anna aimed a spray bottle at the front of the massive stainless refrigerator and doused it in suds before going to work wiping the liquid away.

"No, dear," she replied between swipes. "Always out, but hardly ever home. Not for the longest time. Haven't seen him smile like that in quite some time, either."

"I don't think he was smiling this morning." The words were out before she thought better of them. What was she doing, whining to his housekeeper? "I mean, I think he may have been upset." She winced. How was that any better? She needed to just shut up.

"He was fine, dear. Don't let little things like that get to you. He'll be right as rain the next time you see him, mark my words."

She glanced up to find Anna smiling, her blue eyes twinkling. She had to be seventy, maybe older. What did she know about relationships? But there was something about her. Something wise.

Anna's smile grew wider, and she nodded, as though she were reading Melanie's thoughts.

"I hope you're right," Melanie said.

"And what did you want to ask me, dear?"

Melanie played with her shiny red fingernails. "I sort of owe Taz an apology, so I was thinking I might make him dinner tonight. I was wondering if you could tell me what he likes to eat."

"A romantic dinner!" Anna gushed. "Won't that be grand?"

Melanie smiled. She hoped it would be a good start anyway. If things went well—and if she didn't lose her nerve—it was going to be a lot more than that.

"Mr. Roman enjoys most things," Anna continued. "He's not overly particular. Maybe a little finicky about his meats. And some of his vegetables." She tapped her lip. "Sauces can be difficult." She frowned. "What did you have in mind?"

"I don't know. I was hoping you could suggest something."

Anna brightened. "He has a sweet spot for my stovies. And a deep and hearty Scotch broth." She stopped. "Do you make a good broth?"

Melanie shook her head. "And I don't know what stovies are."

"Oh, they're are delicious. You start with a little tattie, a little mince… oh, never mind that." She reached over and tapped Melanie's hand. "I've just had the grandest idea. Tell me what you think."

CHAPTER FIVE

TAZ'S PHONE JINGLED. He glanced at it sitting on the center console of his Jeep. It was Melanie again. Third time in an hour. He'd meant to call her at the cargo office after he'd finally persuaded the guy at the counter to let him in the warehouse to double check the drum crates. Garrett had assured him shipping the instruments as cargo would be more dependable than checking them as luggage, but he didn't want any surprises when they arrived at Heathrow. He had enough to worry about.

He turned down the stereo, tapped the phone's screen, and waited for the Bluetooth receiver to connect. "Hey, I'm on my way," he said.

"On your way home?"

She sounded surprised. Guess he shouldn't have been. Who knew what she was thinking after he'd ignored her calls and text messages all day?

"I mean, that's great," she added quickly. "I'm already here. Are you close? How much longer, do you think?"

"I'm at Crenshaw, and traffic's pretty light. I'd say twenty minutes, or a little more. He glanced at the dashboard clock. It was nearly eight o'clock. "If you're hungry, feel free to grab something from the kitchen."

"No, I'm fine. I was just wondering. Okay, um, see you soon. Bye."

The line went dead.

He frowned. Was she just hungry? Was she pissed? Probably pissed. Wouldn't he be if she'd avoided him all day? But then he'd been a pretty poor judge of the situation so far.

His fingers tightened on the steering wheel. It still didn't make sense why she didn't want to live with him. She was at his place most of the time anyway. And to think he'd actually thought she would be happy about the idea.

Obviously, he didn't know as much about women as he thought he did—or at least about Melanie. He'd misread her, big time, and it made him wonder what else he'd misread. He didn't want to admit it, but he wasn't looking forward to facing her.

That cringing feeling returned, the one that had dogged him all day and made him think up a dozen little things to do to keep him busy. He must look like an idiot to her now. A needy, lovesick idiot. He should have known better. She'd dumped her last boyfriend for moving too fast, and they'd been together more than a year. And here he was, trying to rope her into a living arrangement after just a few weeks.

Stupid. Stupid. Stupid.

He turned the radio back up, wishing the wild drumbeat could drown out his thoughts. All he could do now was keep busy. He'd keep himself occupied and out of her hair. If she wanted space, he'd make sure she had it. Here and on the road.

His offramp came up, and the muscle in his gut twisted. He just had to play it cool tonight. Once they got on the road, it would be easy to give her space. Sound checks, tech rehearsals, meetings with venue staff, meetings with Garrett, not to mention all the last-minute emergencies that cropped up no matter how much they prepared. He could invent a thousand things to keep his distance.

He just had to play it cool tonight, and he was going to be fine.

CHAPTER SIX

TAZ TURNED INTO his driveway, and pulled up beside Melanie's old Volkswagen Squareback. It was past eight now and the sky and scattered clouds were turning dusky shades of pink and purple as the sun slipped into the horizon. It would have been a perfect night for a walk along the surf, if he hadn't ruined everything this morning.

The streetlights switched on, but the house was dark. Had she given up on him and gone to bed? He wouldn't be surprised. That three a.m. pickup was going to come fast.

He searched his keyring for the house key and opened the door.

Inside it wasn't dark after all. A trail of small, flickering candles led to the patio. And there was Spike, greeting him as she always did with her wiggly happy dance. He set his keys on the foyer table and bent down to greet the dog.

As he rubbed her ears, he noticed the savory smells coming from the kitchen and his stomach grumbled. He was about to investigate when she spoke.

"Welcome home," Melanie said, her voice low and sexy as hell.

He looked around until he found her, just a silhouette standing where the glass doors slid away to reveal the patio filled with more candles, and their reflections twinkling in the infinity pool like stars. Her hair was down, curving gently over one shoulder, and a long, silky white dress hugged every one of her curves.

"It's good to be home," he said, silently kicking himself for not getting home sooner. The aroma from the kitchen tugged at him again. He turned toward it. "What's cooking? It smells amazing." He touched the swinging door.

"Don't go in there," she blurted and hurried across the room.

He stopped. "Why? What's wrong?"

She slid into the space between him and the door. "What I mean is," she said, her voice back to its calm, seductive tone, "dinner's already on the table outside."

She hooked his arm and led him to the patio.

As she closed the sliding-glass door behind them, he paused and took in the tiny white lights she'd strewn above the patio table like a canopy and wound around every post and every potted palm. The table itself was set like a five-star restaurant, with white linen and gleaming silver cloches set over a cozy meal for two.

"You did all this?" he asked. "It's incredible."

CHAPTER SEVEN

MELANIE SQUEEZED TAZ'S arm gently. "I wanted to apologize for this morning. You caught me off guard, and I didn't handle it well. I was an idiot."

He turned to her and leveled his dark green gaze on her. "No, you weren't," he said. "You were just being honest."

His seriousness overwhelmed her. It made her think that maybe she could be truly honest—about the tour, about all his fans and all that temptation. She nearly said so, but what if she said something stupid again? And what if it ruined the surprise she had upstairs? The one that was already giving her fits of doubt.

The surprise she was already beginning to regret.

His gaze burned into her, reminding her he was waiting for her to say something.

She stared at the ground. She stared at the twinkling lights reflected in the pool. Then she spotted Spike, watching them longingly from behind the glass, and she welcomed the distraction.

"Oh, little girl," she cooed as she broke away from Taz and went to the sliding-glass door. She had already opened it to grab the little bundle of chestnut fur when she remembered Anna's warning.

It was too late.

Spike erupted in yips and yaps and darted across the patio. Taz lunged for the dog, but she evaded his grasp in her pursuit of a black, feline blur zooming across the patio.

Melanie watched in horror as the cat leaped onto her meticulously set table, causing a calamity of shattered crystal goblets, red wine, and rose petals, before coming to rest in a queenly pose in the center of the destruction.

Spike growled and tried to leap onto the table. She didn't make it to the top, but she made it far enough to sink her claws into the linen, and she stayed there, suspended, until gravity pulled her and everything that had been on the table clattering to the ground.

The cat leapt away easily and was running toward the fence, with Spike following behind and Taz and Melanie following them both.

Taz took the long way around the pool, and Melanie took the shorter, figuring they would eventually close in on the animals. The cat, seeing their intent, took a shortcut by leaping over the turquoise-tiled divide separating the pool from the hot tub. Spike followed but, unable to jump, she ran headlong across the narrow bridge. Her paws lost their grip on the smooth, wet ceramic tile, and she slipped and careened into the deep end of the pool.

The dog flailed and frantically tried to keep her head above water, yet instead of staying close to the edge, she drifted farther toward the middle.

Melanie was first to reach the side closest to Spike. She kneeled and tried to grab the dog, but her fingertips only brushed her ears. "C'mon, Spike," she urged. "C'mon, girl. This way."

But it was no use. The dog was paddling but still out of reach.

Melanie stretched. If she could just get her finger hooked behind Spike's collar, if she could just lean another inch…

She'd gone too far. She knew it even before the bracing cold water rose up to smack her in the face.

The last thing she heard before her head plunged underwater was Taz yelling to hold on. To what? Certainly not her dignity. That was long gone.

There was no time to wallow in her own cringing embarrassment, though. She bobbed up, found Spike, and scooped the little bundle of shivering wet fur.

She swam to the shallow end and trudged up the pool steps, drenched and covered in goosebumps as the water sluiced off her and little Spike, leaving puddles wherever they went.

Taz raced up to her and wrapped a beach towel around her shoulders. "Are you all right?"

She cradled Spike, whose body shook with cold.

"You need to get her inside and get her warm," Melanie said, shimmying out of the comforting towel and wrapping it around Spike. "She could catch a cold or worse if she stays out here."

"But what about you?" Taz said. "You're soaked."

"I'll take care of me," she said. "You take care of Spike." She handed him the dog and stroked the chestnut head one last time.

"But, Melanie," he said, as she walked away.

She didn't turn back.

CHAPTER EIGHT

MELANIE TRUDGED THROUGH the house, leaving a watery trail behind her. She intended to leave, to take the whole soaking wet mess she'd made of the night and just leave. She would have, too, if she hadn't caught sight of herself in the giant mirror beside the foyer when she went to grab her purse.

She noticed her hair first. The hair she'd so carefully coaxed into a Veronica Lake-like wave over her shoulder was a disaster, plastered against her cheeks and shoulders in wet, stringy hanks. But it was her dress that stopped her in her tracks. Her innocent white halter dress that showed off her shoulder tattoos and her summer tan was now showing off a lot more than that—probably enough to get her arrested if she left the house.

A fresh wave of shame flooded over her.

She veered from the front door and went to the small bathroom beside the staircase. Inside, she grabbed a folded paper towel from the basket beside the sink and dabbed at her chest. Instantly the paper saturated and turned into a wet ball of tissue. She grabbed a fistful of the paper towels, tried again, and found herself holding an even bigger wet ball. She threw it in the trash bin, leaned against the door, and laughed.

Of course everything went wrong. What did she expect? This was her life, this is what happened to her. Just because she'd miraculously tricked fate and found herself in the Belly Dance Divas dance company and somehow convinced Taz she was worth his time for a few weeks, it didn't mean anything was different. Her luck was bound to run out. A second-hand meal, a few measly candles and twinkly lights, and that last gasp of desperation upstairs wasn't going to change that.

Nothing had changed.

She laughed again, and she'd keep laughing until the pain went away.

CHAPTER NINE

TAZ WAS IN the kitchen, rubbing Spike with a fourth dishtowel when he heard laughter coming from the bathroom.

It wasn't Melanie's usual laugh, the infectious peal that always made him smile. This was something else. Something dark and bleak. It worried him. He set Spike in the window-seat cushion with her name embroidered into it and tucked more dry dishtowels around her.

"Stay here, Spikey," he whispered.

He left the dog with another rub on the head and went to the closed bathroom door. He paused and listened. Only the whir of the fan. Somehow that worried him more than the ominous laughter. He knocked.

"Melanie, you okay? Do you need anything?"

No response, but he could hear the faucet turn on, then off.

"I just need a minute," she said finally, "then I'll get out of your hair."

He didn't like the sound of that. He tried the door, but it was locked.

"Melanie, what's wrong? Please come out and talk to me. Just let me explain."

The door flew open, and she was there, her brown eyes wide and flashing, and her wet dress clinging to her like a second skin. His words stopped, and his gaze locked on the sight. Every thought vanished but one: That dress.

But it wasn't exactly the dress, or how wet it was or how it clung to her incredible body. It was all of it. A surge of desire overtook him, and his breath caught hard in his throat.

"You have nothing to explain," she said. "I'm the one who ruined everything with my big, stupid mouth. I'm the one who ran you off this morning. Not that I blame you. I'd run away from me, too. I'm a wreck—"

He couldn't help himself. His desire to comfort gave way to his straight-up desire for her. It was too much. Her standing in front of him like that, every inch of her soft, supple body revealed beneath that wet, transparent dress that gave her skin a mesmerizing, glistening sheen. He scooped her into his arms mid-sentence and stopped her mouth with a kiss.

She tensed at the force of him, but slowly, she yielded, relaxing into his embrace.

She wound her arms around his neck and through the hair that brushed over his shoulders. She pressed herself against him, and a shiver ran through him at the feel of the wet fabric—at the cold or the excitement, maybe both.

He pulled back, trying to marshal his thoughts. "You must be freezing."

She licked her reddened lips and bit the edge. "Are you suggesting I get out of these wet clothes?"

Man, he liked the sound of that. A fresh wave of desire flooded over him. "I guess I am."

She pulled her arms from his neck and wound them behind her own. In a moment, the straps of her halter were loose, held in place only by her own arms. He could feel her eyes on him as he watched the halter slip slowly down over the swell of her breasts.

His breath came quick. His heart pounded in his chest. She was playing with him, teasing him with this slow-motion strip tease.

Was it possible to want a woman any more than he wanted her now? When the anticipation was too much, he pushed her against the door jamb, planted his palms on her and slipped the soaking wet fabric down to her waist. He buried his face in the warm hollow of her neck and breathed in her scent. Even mingled with the chlorine and soap, he could smell her. He kissed her soft, slippery skin before descending down over her freshly liberated breasts.

He took one of the rosy pink nipples that had taunted him from beneath that dress between his lips and ran his tongue over the tip until it became a tight, hot knot.

Melanie released a kittenish whimper, and it seared him like a flame. He couldn't wait another moment. He put one arm behind her back and one beneath her knees and lifted her. When she was nestled in his embrace, he met her gaze and with his eyes he asked, Is this all right?

Her eyes gave him the same answer she whispered in two breathless syllables: Take me.

CHAPTER TEN

THE WORDS HAD barely passed her lips when Taz was in action, carrying her up the stairs and down the hallway. When they crossed the threshold to his bedroom, he set her gently at the edge of the bed. She looked up. He was watching her with a long and loaded gaze. She could feel a conversation wrestling within him and it plucked at her regrets. There were so many things they had to say—important and difficult things that needed to be said—but not now.

Right now, she could pretend everything was just as it had been yesterday. That he still felt the same about her. That nothing had changed. She knew it was a lie. All this was just a fleeting surge of hormones and leftover passion, but it was enough.

She took his hands in her own and looked at them. She adored these hands. So big and strong and rough, yet capable of such tenderness. She lifted them to her face, held them to her cheeks, and focused on his pulse. It drummed away her thoughts. Waves of desire filled their place and this determination: If this was going to be her last moments with these hands, with this incredible man, she was going to make the most of it.

She nuzzled his hands again, then guided them down over the hard angle of her jaw, over the slope of her neck. Down around the sides of her breasts, lingering on the soft curve beneath her nipples, that place that always mesmerized him when they made love.

His sharp inhalation told her this time was no different. His arousal fueled her own, and, feeling bolder, she let go of his hands and rose in front of him. His eyes widened, watching her, waiting for her next move. A sly, seductive smile curled on her lips as she pushed the bunched up tube of her dress to her ankles. She stepped out of the wet circle and, now entirely naked, she descended again to the bed.

Still he watched.

"What do you want?" he whispered, his voice rough with desire.

She wanted so many things. She wanted that look never to end. She wanted to memorize the feeling of his touch. She wanted to give him everything.

And then she knew...

"I want you to watch," she whispered back.

His puzzled look lasted only until she leaned back and pulled her feet up onto the bed. She could feel his desire spike with seismic force as her fingers brushed slowly down over her belly.

She wasn't surprised. When they made love, he would try to persuade her to keep the light on or angle himself so he could see the most intimate parts of her. She never let him. Being exposed like that—so bare and so vulnerable—ruined the mood, she'd say. He never pushed, but she knew it was something he wanted.

And she could see by the flush on his cheeks how much he wanted it now.

He caressed her knee, the only part of her he could reach, and she moaned at the warmth radiating through his fingertips.

"Don't stop," he whispered.

"I won't," she whispered back with another smile.

She held his gaze and lowered her hand farther. His gaze followed. When she found her smooth, soft cleft, she dipped one fingertip between and closed her eyes at the familiar tingle and braced for the roaring, urgent need for more. Slowly, she pressed harder and circled the spot, and rocked her hips gently.

She moaned again, or had he? She didn't know because she was floating on a cloud of delicious sensation, aware of nothing but the hungry pulse that began at that delicate part of her and traveled out to every extremity.

When she had nearly brought herself to the pinnacle, she cracked open her eyes to see him watching, his gaze trained on her fingers working at the epicenter of her pleasure.

He released the grip on her knee, then his hand was at his jeans, popping the riveted button and lowering the zipper. With a thud the heavy denim fell to the floor and he was standing in snug, black cotton jockeys, stretched almost beyond belief. He tugged and yanked at the fabric until he was as naked as she was.

The sight of him was more than she could bear. Her own touch no longer satisfied. She reached out her hand. He took it, and she pulled him toward her. He read her body language perfectly, and joined her on the bed, letting her guide his fingertips to where she ached for him.

A moan escaped his lips when he touched her slippery heat, and she pressed her hips against the incredible sensation.

Lifting her arms over her head, she squeezed the silky comforter. She squeezed until her hands were hard, red fists. It was an exquisite agony, at once incredible and terrible, both battling within her until she thought she'd go mad. She wanted him to stop, and she never wanted him to stop.

Each time she determined to pull away, she remembered she might never be here again. Might never feel him again. It made her choice clear: she'd endure anything.

It was impossible to know how long that mad pleasure lasted. Ten minutes, an hour, two? She squirmed and whimpered through one orgasm after another until time seemed irrelevant. Only when she felt him pull away was she roused from his spell.

Was it over? Was it done? She was about to beg for more when she realized he wasn't finished at all.

He was crawling up onto the bed beside her and then he was on top of her, stroking her hair with one hand and maneuvering himself between her legs with the other.

She closed her eyes, immersing herself in the relief that mingled with her hunger for more.

"Watch me," he whispered.

She opened her eyes and found him staring deeply into hers.

"Don't close them," he whispered. "I want to see you. I want you to see me."

She wasn't sure what that meant. He'd never asked for that before, but tonight they were exploring all kinds of new territory, and his tone told her it meant plenty to him. She locked her gaze on his. Even when he pressed into her, filling her completely and bringing her to the brink of a scream, she didn't close her eyes. She bit her lip, she gasped for air, she clutched her fingernails into his back, but she didn't close her eyes.

And then it came. They both did, because when she recognized that final flush of passion in his expression, that sharp tensing of his limbs, and the primal moan that escaped his lips, it didn't matter that her body had endured more tonight than she'd ever endured before and that she was sure she would collapse into an exhausted heap at any moment, feeling him reach his release triggered another of her own, and it shook her to her core.

At the end, she was beyond the point of exhaustion, beyond thought or even regret. She closed her eyes and committed every sensation to memory: the weight of his thigh on hers, his fingers cupping her breast, his breath on neck. She collected it all and held it tight. She held it like she'd never let it go.

CHAPTER ELEVEN

TAZ COULDN'T MOVE, he could hardly breathe, but his mind was racing. Sex had never been boring with Melanie, but that was something else.

Did it mean she forgave him?

Maybe they could just forget what an idiot he'd been and move on.

No, he couldn't play it that way. She might let him, but it wouldn't be right. She deserved better.

"Before I got so distracted," he said, trying to keep the mood light, "I wanted to apologize for this morning. I wasn't thinking. I know you don't want to rush into another relationship. And there's the tour, and hell, I didn't even think about everything you're going through with your mom. So, I just wanted to say I'm sorry."

She turned to face him. "You're sorry?"

Was that disbelief or sarcasm in her voice?

"Yeah," he said tentatively. "Why does that surprise you?"

She bolted upright. He tried to concentrate, but the way her breasts jiggled at the abrupt movement made him hungry for her all over again.

"Well, yeah," she said, "considering you have nothing to be sorry for. I do. I was an idiot. I always have a way of saying exactly the wrong thing, and then I tried to make it up to you with this stupid romantic dinner, and I really should have known better. I suck at the romantic stuff. Hey, buddy, eyes up here, okay? I'm trying to apologize."

His eyes shot up. "Sorry, but when you move and they sway, just like... forget it." He forced the image of her breasts from his mind. What had she been saying? He replayed her words, and this time they sank in.

But they didn't make sense.

"You did all that because you thought I was mad at you? The dinner and the lights, everything?"

"The aquatic show at the end wasn't exactly part of the plan, but, yeah, I wanted it to be special, before we leave. And before everything changes."

"What's going to change? Nothing's going to change." He sat up and put his hand on hers.

"Of course it will. We're going out on the road. You're going to have women throwing themselves at you after every show. You're going to have belly dancers throwing themselves at you during the show. How can you say nothing's going to change?"

"Is that what you think it's like? Because it's not. It's just like it is here: you perform, you go to a party—okay, maybe there's some flirting at the parties—but it doesn't matter because you're exhausted and you have to get some sleep before you have to get up early to get to the next city, or to a sound check, or to a radio station, or to whatever insane marketing thing Garrett has set up. And none of that even matters anyway because there's you, Melanie."

He reached out and guided a loose strand of her hair back behind her ear. "You change everything. You're the only one I want."

CHAPTER TWELVE

MELANIE WANTED TO believe him. She realized she wanted him more than anything.

"Are you sure?" she asked, knowing how weak and vulnerable she sounded, but she didn't care. She had to know.

"I asked you to move in with me this morning. I don't think it gets more serious than that."

"But—"

"Don't worry," he interrupted. "I'm not pushing. I can wait until you're ready. But speaking of ready," he glanced at the clock. It was past midnight. "I'm not trying to get rid of you, but I didn't see your suitcase downstairs so I assume you need to run back to your mom's place to get it. Our airport ride is going to be here in just a few hours."

She sighed but didn't say anything.

"You do have to go back to your mom's for your things, don't you?"

She shook her head and wondered if she was about to make another huge mistake. One she wouldn't be able to undo.

"Why not?"

"It's not there."

He frowned. "Where did it go?"

There was no backing out now. She had to tell him what she'd done. She pulled a sheet off the bed and wrapped it around herself, then took his hand. "You should come with me."

He let her pull him out of the room and down the hall to the guest bedroom. She opened the closed door and waited for his reaction.

"Huh," he said matter-of-factly and rubbed at the golden stubble accumulating on his chin.

"It's not everything," she said, staring at the suitcase, three cardboard boxes, and two grocery bags filled with her clothes and necessities that were piled on the bed. "There are still some things at my mom's."

"What about your mom?"

"Turns out," she said, "she's tougher than I thought. She doesn't need me. In fact, I think she wants her extra room back."

He nodded, taking it in. "And the suitcase, that's for the tour?"

"Yeah."

"And the rest of it?"

"I was kinda hoping this morning's offer was still good, and that you'd let me move into your home." Whatever was left of the confidence she'd built up melted beneath his inscrutable gaze. She reminded herself to be strong. This morning she'd convinced herself the worst that could happen was he'd say no and she'd have to pack her stuff back into her car. Now she feared it could do—or undo—so much more.

He slipped his hand in hers and pulled her against him.

"Of course," he said. "But you've got it wrong. This isn't my home."

Her breath caught. So that was how he was going to play it. He was going to tell her some bullshit about his sister being a part owner or make some other lame excuse. She wanted to undo it all. She wanted to run.

He tightened his hold on her hand. "I thought it was, all these years. But since I've been with you, I realize it's only a building. It's only a house. You're my home, Melanie. Whether we're here, or in a hotel, or anywhere in the world, it doesn't matter. I'm home when I'm with you. I love you, Melanie."

She couldn't believe he was saying these things to her, or that he felt this way. She wanted to respond, to say anything really, but the words locked in her throat. Instead she threw her arms around him and buried her head in his neck.

He wrapped his arms around her and stroked her hair.

When she could finally speak, she pulled back. "I love you, too. You have no idea how much I want to be with you. You're so good and wonderful, but I'm... not. I haven't been completely honest, and you deserve to know the truth before this goes any further."

He frowned, waiting.

"I didn't cook the meal that's splattered all over your patio—and which I'm going to help you clean up, by the way. But you should know I can't cook anything, so if you're hoping for some kind of super-Susie Q homemaker who's going to have dinner ready for you every night, we might as well—"

He stopped her with a kiss, a long, sweet, strong kiss that curled her toes and left her breathless.

When he pulled away, he lifted her chin with his finger and said, simply, "I know."

"You do?"

"I know Anna cooked that dinner, if that's what you mean."

"You knew all along?"

He nodded with a smug smile.

"You couldn't. I made her promise not to tell you, and she cleaned up everything, every pot and pan."

"Beef Bourguignon with tons of tiny onions, right? Fingerling potatoes? And crusty bread to soak up the sauce?"

She was speechless. It was the menu exactly.

He chuckled. "It's Anna's favorite, and she always uses three times more pepper in the sauce than anybody I know. I could smell it the second I walked in."

She crossed her arms in a huff. "Busted by peppery Bourguignon."

He laughed.

"I think I know what will make you feel better."

She wiggled her eyebrows. "Really?"

"Anna always cooks enough to feed an army. Somewhere in my fridge is a stash of leftovers that I promise will taste every bit as good as what's out there." He jutted his thumb toward the patio.

She lowered her lids and wiggled her shoulders seductively. "Oh, baby, you know what I like."

"Careful," he said, scooping her up in his arms. "Or you're going to start something."

"Promises, promises," she said. "The car's going to be here in just a few hours, and we still have a patio to clean up."

"Really? How about you tell me about it in the bedroom?" He pulled her back and planted another kiss on her lips.

She purred in his ear, "With pleasure."

THE END

***

Have you read all the books in the *California Belly Dance Romance* series?

Shimmy for Me (Book 1)
Dance with Me (Book 2)
Another Dance (Book 3)
Jingly Bells (Book 4)

Visit www.DeAnnaCameron.com for details

AUTHOR'S NOTE

Thank you for taking the time to read *Another Dance.*

If you enjoyed it, please consider leaving a review at your favorite e-retailer or Goodreads.com. Your support makes a real difference and would be truly appreciated.

If you'd like to know more about me, please visit my website at www.DeAnnaCameron.com.

ACKNOWLEDGMENTS

I'd like to thank some special people who contributed in important ways to this book:

The members of the Extraordinary Readers Club, who keep me inspired and motivated: Jasmine Talbert, Shannon, Michelle, Ann Johnson, Nikki, Laura, Christina, Jennifer, Abigail, Clarissa, Tracy, and Alice.

Robert Crane, for his eagle eyes and steadfast support.

My friends and family, who continually amaze me with their support and encouragement, and love. hero.

www.ingramcontent.com/pod-product-compliance
Lightning Source LLC
Chambersburg PA
CBHW020601130626
46552CB00007B/2995